Squanto's Journey

THE STORY OF THE FIRST THANKSGIVING

Joseph Bruchac
ILLUSTRATED BY Greg Shed

VOYAGER BOOKS · HARCOURT, INC.

ORLANDO   AUSTIN   NEW YORK   SAN DIEGO   TORONTO   LONDON   PRINTED IN CHINA

MY STORY IS BOTH STRANGE AND TRUE. I was born in the year the English call 1590. My family were leaders of the Patuxet people and I, too, was raised to lead. But in 1614 I was taken to Spain against my will. Now it is 1621 and I am again in my homeland. My name is Squanto. I would like to tell you my tale.

I look up and watch a heron flying overhead. It goes toward the falls that gave our people their name. We were the Patuxet, the People of the Falls. Our cleared fields were not empty of people then as they were when the English pilgrims landed in the Freezing Moon of 1620. Only six winters have passed, but so many things have changed.

I remember that day in 1614. White men had come often to fish in our bay and trade. They had brought us fine things in exchange for beaver and deerskins. This time—when their tall ships, with sails like the wings of giant birds, anchored offshore—this time was different.

John Smith was one of the English captains. He and his officer, Thomas Dermer, traded with us. I liked the way Dermer shook my hand. Smith had learned much from dealing with other Indians in the summer land of Virginia. He knew we valued honor.

The other captain was Thomas Hunt. After Smith left, Hunt landed at Patuxet. He told us he was Smith's friend. "Come to a feast on my ship," he said.

More than twenty of us went aboard to share food with friends. But Hunt was no friend. He set sail, taking us with him as captives. Left behind were our families, our homes, our people. Our lives were no longer our own.

Soon we were crossing the wide salt waters. The journey was long, but my spirit did not desert me. I remembered I was *pniese,* a man of courage. I told stories to my people and urged them to stay strong.

Hunt took us to Malaga in the land of Spain. There we were sold to be slaves. But men who serve the Creator lived there. It was they, who called themselves Brothers, who freed us from our chains.

I learned more of their language. I let them teach me about their ways of thanking the Great Mystery. I told them what I wanted most. I wanted to return home. With the Friars' help, I went to England. English ships often sailed toward the sunset. I realized that if I could be of use to the English, they might take me with them.

It took much work, but I learned the language well. In March of the year they call 1619, I sailed back to New England at the side of my friend Thomas Dermer, one of John Smith's officers. Our memories of each other were like the taste of good water. He told me that things were not well between my People of the First Light and the English. Englishmen and their ships were now being attacked when they came to shore. Perhaps if I accompanied the English, I could speak with the Indians and they could trade again in peace. My heart felt as if it were soaring on an eagle's wings as the ship cut through the waves. But I also feared what I might find.

"Where there were this many people," he said, telling me of great illness in New England brought on by white traders, "now only this many remain." He folded back all but two fingers.

It proved as he said. The sickness had come down upon Patuxet like the blow of a war club. Only a few of my people survived. My wife, my children, my parents, and all those closest to me were gone. I will not say their names now. I will speak them again when my own feet climb the highest mountain and I walk the Road of Stars to greet them.

Together, Thomas Dermer and I did our work. We made friendly contact with the Nemasket and Pokanoket. More than once, my words saved the life of my English friend. Peace seemed within our reach.

But Epanow, the powerful sachem of Capawack, viewed the English as one might a deadly serpent. Epanow, too, had been taken to England as a slave and brought back to act as a guide. He had escaped and vowed to always fight the white men. The deeds of other Englishmen convinced his people that he was right. In the summer of 1620, as Thomas Dermer and I talked of peace, an English captain invited a party of Indians on board their ship. Then suddenly, the white men shot them down.

When we reached the island of Capawack, Epanow and his warriors attacked us. Many English were killed. Thomas Dermer was wounded. With my help he was able to escape, but I was taken captive and given to the Pokanoket as a prisoner.

That November, when the *Mayflower* reached shore, the Pokanoket watched. They did not come close to the English. If the Pokanoket had been stronger, they might have attacked the white men—wiped them out or driven them away. But the Pokanoket were still weak from the great sickness. Where there had been thousands, now there were hundreds.

The strength of our people was so small now that the Narragansett to the south, untouched by the plague themselves, ordered the once-proud Pokanoket and Nemasket to pay them tribute.

I spoke to Massasoit, the sachem of the Pokanoket, as a *pniese* should, with respect and honor. "Befriend the English," I said. "Make them come to understand and support our people."

Massasoit did not listen at first. He watched silently through that winter.

Then Samoset came to visit. He was a sachem of the Pemaquid people, who lived farther up the coast. He had done much trading with the English. He knew some of their language.

"Let me talk with the Songlismoniak," he said to Massasoit, nodding to me as he spoke. Massasoit agreed.

The next day, March 16th of 1621, Samoset strode into the English settlement.

"Welcome, English," he said in their tongue. He showed them the two arrows in his hand. One had a flint arrowhead, the other had the arrowhead removed. The arrows symbolized what we offered them, either war or peace.

The English placed a coat about his shoulders to warm him. They invited him into one of their houses. They gave him small water, biscuits and butter, pudding and cheese.

"The food was so good," Samoset said to me later, laughing as he spoke, "I decided to spend the night."

When he left the next day, he promised to return with a friend who spoke their language well.

So it was that five days later, on the 22nd of March, I walked with Samoset back into my own village. Once Patuxet, now it was Plymouth. I looked around me. Though much was changed, I knew that I at last had returned to the land of my home.

"Perhaps these men can share our land as friends," I told my brother, at my side.

In the moons that followed, there was much work to do. The Pokanoket freed me to be a guide and interpreter for the English. Not only did I act as envoy between the English and our people, I also had many things to teach the white people about survival. They knew little of hunting and almost nothing of planting. It had always been the job of the Patuxet women to care for the crops while men such as myself hunted. But I had observed much in the years since my captivity. I had seen in Newfoundland how the English learned from our people how to grow corn.

"Use the small fish that wash up on our shores in great numbers," I told the English. "Bury those fish in the earth and they will feed the corn."

I showed them how to plant the seeds of corn and beans and squash together in hills. I told them when it was the Moon of Hoeing. They listened well and worked hard. I came to see that these pilgrims could be our friends and we theirs. Together we might make our home on this land given to us by the Creator of All Things.

A good harvest was brought in this fall. Some of their English crops have not done well. But the three sisters—the corn and beans and squash—have done well. As I look at the beans, growing up about the stalks of the corn, I think of how our two people have become entwined. I feel hope for our children in the seasons to come. With our help, the English have learned enough of hunting and fishing to provide the food for a great feast such as this one—this feast for all our people.

Now as we eat together, I give thanks. I have seen more in my life than most men, whether Indian or English. I have seen both death and life come to this land that gives itself to English and Indian alike. I pray that there will be many more such days to give thanks together in the years that follow.

I am Squanto. I am known to all those who gather here: English, Pokanoket, Nemasket, even a few of my own surviving Patuxets. I speak to you as a *pniese*, a man of honor. I will never leave this land. I give thanks for all of our people to the Creator of All Things.

Author's Note

The story of the Pilgrims and the first Thanksgiving Day is familiar to every child in America. However, the Native American side of that tale is seldom told. I've always been fascinated by the role played by Native Americans—and especially the man known as Tisquantum or Squanto—in helping that first New England colony survive.

Squanto's is a tale that I think is inspiring to both Native and non-Native readers alike. Not only did Squanto escape from slavery in Spain and make influential friends in England, but he was able to find his way back home. Even though his closest family and friends had died from a plague introduced by the English, he became the interpreter and guide for the Pilgrims. It is no exaggeration to say that without Squanto, the Plymouth colony might have failed. Squanto's journey is an incredible saga of both survival and acceptance. He was one of the first Native Americans to live successfully in the worlds of both the European and the Indian. As a person of Native American New England descent myself, Squanto's story has a special reverberation for me.

However, being Indian does not mean that you automatically know about all things Native American. Whenever I tell a story that comes from another Native nation, it is my responsibility to hear the living voices of those Native people. One of my first inspirations for this story was my late friend Nanepashemet, a Wampanoag scholar and historical interpreter, an academic and traditionalist respected in both worlds. Nanepashemet worked for many years at Plimoth Plantation, the living history museum of the original Massachussetts colony. The accuracy and relaxed, very Indian atmosphere of the Wampanoag village that now stands next to Plimoth Plantation is due to the integrity and commitment of such people as Nanepashemet. His own historical novel about Squanto is now being edited by Linda Coombs, another prominent Wampanoag scholar and defender of their nation's traditions. *Squanto's Journey* could not have been written without their work and the contributions of other contemporary Wampanoag people such as Russell Peters (Fast Turtle), the late John Peters (Slow Turtle), and many others who continue to stand and speak for the people. *Wliwini nidobak!* (Thank you, my friends.)

I also thank my sister Marge Bruchac for her extensive research into the true story of Tisquantum and the everyday lives of the Pilgrims and the Wampanoag people of the early seventeenth century. Virtually every telling of the first Thanksgiving story is marred by historical errors in the depictions of the event, from the food served at the feast to the clothing worn by the Pilgrims (not hats with buckles on them!). Whenever I write a story dealing with New England Native history, I always turn first to Marge, who has been consulted by numerous historical villages, museums, and Indian nations, including Old Sturbridge Village, the Mohegan Tribe, Historic Northampton, and Plimoth Plantation.

Then there is the land itself. Our Native people have always believed that the land talks to us when we listen. I have stood on the same ground where Squanto walked three centuries ago, feeling the sea breeze in my face and smelling the smoke from cooking fires, where the same foods he would have eaten were being cooked in the traditional way. As I stood there, I, too, heard the whisper of the earth, a song on the wind reminding me that those ancient voices will never be gone.

To my Wampanoag brothers and sisters

—J. B.

To Kat (Lakota Nation), Cheyenne (Lakota and Tongva Nations), Steven (Tongva Nation), James Red Bear (Lakota Nation), and David

—G. S.

GLOSSARY

Patuxet: One of the divisions of the Wampanoag peoples, literally "People of the Falls."

pniese: A Wampanoag man who has been initiated. A *pniese* is expected to be a man of great honor and courage who may act as an adviser to his nation.

Pokanoket: One of the divisions of the Wampanoag peoples, literally "People of the Cleared Land."

Road of Stars: The Milky Way, which is seen as a trail to reach the afterlife walked by those who have died.

sachem: A leader of the people.

small water: A drink prepared by the pilgrims.

Songlismoniak: The word *Englishmen* as it is said in Wabanaki.

Wampanoag: The overall name applied to a number of related native peoples in the area of present-day Massachusetts. Literal translation is "People of the First Light."

For information about permission to reproduce selections from this book, write to trade.permissions@hmhco.com or to Permissions, Houghton Mifflin Harcourt Publishing Company, 3 Park Avenue, 19th Floor, New York, New York 10016.

www.hmhco.com

First Voyager Books edition 2007

Voyager Books is a trademark of Harcourt, Inc., registered in the United States of America and/or other jurisdictions.

The Library of Congress has cataloged the hardcover edition as follows:
Bruchac, Joseph.
Squanto's journey: the story of the first Thanksgiving/Joseph Bruchac; illustrated by Greg Shed.
p.   cm.
Summary: Squanto recounts how in 1614 he was captured by the British, sold into slavery in Spain, and ultimately returned to the New World to become a guide and friend for the colonists.
1. Squanto—Juvenile Fiction.   2. Wampanoag Indians—Juvenile Fiction.
[1. Squanto—Fiction.   2. Wampanoag Indians—Fiction.   3. Indians of North America—Massachusetts—Fiction.   4. Pilgrims (New Plymouth Colony)—Fiction.]
I. Shed, Greg, ill.   II. Title.
PZ7.B82816Sq   2000
[Fic]—dc21   99-12012
ISBN 978-0-15-201817-7
ISBN 978-0-15-206044-2 pb

SCP   20 19 18 17
4500690651

The illustrations in this book were done in gouache.
The display type was set in Caslon Antique.
The text type was set in Fournier.
Printed by RR Donnelley China
Production supervision by Christine Witnik
Designed by Kaelin Chappell